# MARY-KATE AND ASHLEY in ACTION!

## Password: Red Hot

A novelization by Kristen Pettit
based on the teleplay
by Robin Riordan

HarperEntertainment
*An Imprint of* HarperCollins*Publishers*

A PARACHUTE PRESS BOOK

W9-CEE-463

A PARACHUTE PRESS BOOK

Parachute Publishing, L.L.C.
156 Fifth Avenue, Suite 302
New York, NY 10010

Published by
HarperEntertainment
*An Imprint of* HarperCollins*Publishers*
10 East 53rd Street, New York, NY 10022-5299

Visit the on-line book boutique on the World Wide Web at
www.mary-kateandashley.com.

Visit HarperEntertainment on the World Wide Web at
www.harpercollins.com

10 9 8 7 6 5 4 3 2 1

# CHAPTER ONE
# Fun in the Sun

"Surf's up, Ashley!" Mary-Kate shouted to her sister. She picked up her surfboard and ran for the water.

"Hey!" Ashley cried. "Wait for me!" She grabbed her own board and hurried across the sand.

*Splash!* Ashley jumped into the water. She and Mary-Kate paddled their boards way out into the deep blue Pacific Ocean.

*Vacationing in Hawaii is the best,* Ashley thought. *Sun, fun—and no secret missions!*

Not many people knew it, but Mary-Kate and Ashley were special agents. They worked for a top secret organization called Headquarters. Their job was to protect the world from evil villains! But this week, Mary-Kate and Ashley were off duty.

Ashley bobbed up and down on the water. "These swells are amazing!" she cried.

"Time to ride the waves," Mary-Kate called.

The girls stood up on their boards. Ashley glided through a curl.

"Excellent!" Ashley cried. She pumped her fist in the air.

"Hey, check me out!" Mary-Kate said.

Ashley looked at her sister. Mary-Kate was standing on one leg!

"That's nothing," Ashley said. "Try this!" She bent down and rested her hands on the board. Then she lifted her feet. A perfect handstand!

Mary-Kate and Ashley rode the wave all the way to the white sandy beach. Then they hopped off their boards.

Ashley smiled. "Looks like Quincy found us some seats." She pointed toward three colorful beach chairs. Quincy, the girls' beige Scottie, was lying on one of the chairs. He had on black sunglasses.

The girls hurried over to Quincy. They planted their boards in the sand and sat down on the beach chairs. "What a great vacation!" Ashley said. "Those waves are awesome."

"Yeah," Mary-Kate agreed. "You have to love those northwest waves."

"Northwest, southeast, who cares?" Ashley asked. "As long as they're huge. Right, Quincy?"

Quincy lowered his sunglasses with one paw. "Actually, Mary-Kate is right. Northwest waves are the largest."

"Shhh!" Mary-Kate said. "No one is supposed to know that you can talk, remember?"

"Don't worry," Ashley put in. "There's no one around."

To everyone else, Quincy looked like an ordinary dog. But he was really a high-tech robot! He helped Mary-Kate and Ashley on all their missions. He also helped them with their homework!

"You should have known about the northwest waves," Quincy told Ashley. "They were in your astronomy textbook. Chapter Five."

Quincy pushed a beach bag toward Ashley with his nose. Ashley peeked inside the bag. Right on top was her astronomy textbook.

"Come on, Quincy," Ashley moaned. "This is our vacation! Why do we have to learn about outer space?"

"We're on vacation only from our special agent jobs," Mary-Kate said, "not from our homework."

"You're just saying that because you already did your homework," Ashley grumbled. She sighed and picked up her textbook.

Ashley opened the book and read a page. "Hey, did you guys know that stars are balls of burning gas? And that stars

produce heat? In fact, our very own sun
is a star!"

Mary-Kate shook her head. "My sister
the encyclopedia!"

Ashley laughed. It was true. She loved
learning all sorts of interesting facts. She
never knew when one would come in
handy during a secret mission!

Ashley scanned the next page. Suddenly,

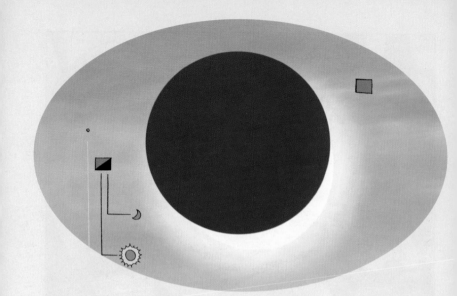

a dark shadow fell over the book. "Whoa! Who dimmed the lights?" she asked.

Ashley glanced up and saw something large and round pass in front of the sun. "What is that?"

"It's a partial eclipse!" Mary-Kate said. "Something in outer space is blocking the sun."

"According to my internal computer, there should not be an eclipse today," Quincy reported.

"That's weird," Ashley said. "What do you think is happening?"

"Whatever it is, it can't be good," Mary-Kate replied.

Ashley sighed. "Does this mean what I think it means?" she asked. "Is our vacation about to be cut short?"

"I'm afraid so," a voice said. Ashley turned to see her friend Rodney Choy standing behind her beach chair. Rod also worked for Headquarters. His job was to drive Mary-Kate and Ashley wherever they needed to go.

"Headquarters just called," Rod went on. "It's time to get back to work!"

# CHAPTER TWO
## On the Case

"So what's the deal?" Ashley asked as Rod drove his Jeep along the winding roads. "Why did Headquarters cancel our vacation?"

"I'm not sure, but it sounds really serious," Rod answered. "Ivan will have all the info by the time we reach your jet."

Fifteen-year-old Ivan Quintero also worked at Headquarters. He made special-agent gadgets for the girls to use on their missions. The girls nicknamed him IQ.

Rod turned into the local airport. He drove the Jeep up a ramp and into Mary-Kate and Ashley's private jet. Inside, the jet looked like a house! IQ was waiting for them in the living room.

"Sorry to drag you away from the beach," IQ said, "but we've got an emergency. Headquarters informs me that someone is trying to block out the sun!"

"So we need to figure out who it is?" Mary-Kate asked.

"Actually, we already know who it is." IQ pushed a button on his computer. A picture of a man blinked onto the screen.

Ashley studied the picture. The man had thin silvery hair and dark narrow eyes. Ashley knew that face very well. "It's Clive Hedgemorton-Smythe," she said.

"How did you know that?" Rod asked.

"We've stopped him from taking over the world before," Mary-Kate said.

IQ nodded. "Lately, Clive has been buying tons of astronomy equipment. Your job is to travel to England, find out Clive's evil plan, and stop him from blocking out the sun." IQ handed Mary-Kate the case file.

"And fast," Rod added. "Because if Clive is able to block out the sun, the world will freeze. Life on Earth will come to an end!"

Ashley gasped. A frozen planet? This was *beyond* serious.

"We're on the case," Mary-Kate said. "Now show us the new special-agent toys."

Ashley smiled. Mary-Kate *loved* the gadgets that IQ invented for them.

IQ handed Mary-Kate and Ashley two chunky bracelets. "Here are your special-agent bracelets. As usual, they have a telephone, a digital diary, and a compass."

"Excellent." Mary-Kate strapped her bracelet to her wrist. She pressed a button on the side and began to speak. "Digital diary: Twelve P.M. We are ready to stop Clive from turning the Earth into a giant ice cube."

"I also have a new way for the two of you to talk to each other if you're separated," IQ added.

He reached into the pocket of his lab coat and pulled out a tube of lipstick and a pair of earrings. Then he put on one of the earrings.

Ashley giggled. "No offense, IQ, but you're *not* the earring type."

IQ blushed. "It's not a real earring. It's a receiver for your new lipstick microphones." He handed the lipstick to Ashley. "If you speak into the lipstick, whoever is wearing the earrings will hear you."

"Testing!" Ashley shouted into the lipstick.

IQ grabbed his ear. "Ouch!" he cried.

"Oops, sorry," Ashley said.

"Looks like we're ready to go," Mary-Kate said. "Fire up the jet, Rod. I'm flying us to England!"

"No way," Ashley said. "It's *my* turn to fly."

"No, it's *my* turn," Mary-Kate said.

"Girls," Quincy said. "There's only one way to settle this fairly."

Ashley shrugged. "Rock-paper-scissors?"

Mary-Kate nodded. "One, two, three—go!"

Ashley made a tight fist. "Rock!"

At the same time, Mary-Kate spread out her hand. "Paper!"

Ashley groaned.

"Paper covers rock! I win!" Mary-Kate cheered. "Say good-bye to Hawaii. Jolly old England, here we come!"

# CHAPTER THREE
## Just Dropping In

Mary-Kate and Ashley's jet zoomed through the sky.

As Mary-Kate handled the controls,

Ashley flipped through Headquarters's file on Clive Hedgemorton-Smythe. She wanted to review all the facts about the villain before she met him again.

"Clive Hedgemorton-Smythe. Originally born in Cheddar," Ashley read from the file.

"Cheddar? Like the cheese?" Mary-Kate asked.

Ashley shrugged. "I guess. Although we know he likes to eat Stilton."

"What's Stilton?" Rod asked. He was sitting behind the cockpit, controlling the jet's radio system.

"English cheese," Mary-Kate explained. "It's *really* stinky."

Ashley continued to read the file. "Clive now lives in his family's mansion. The mansion is called Hedgemoor Manor."

Rod pressed his headset to his ears. "We're cleared for landing, girls!"

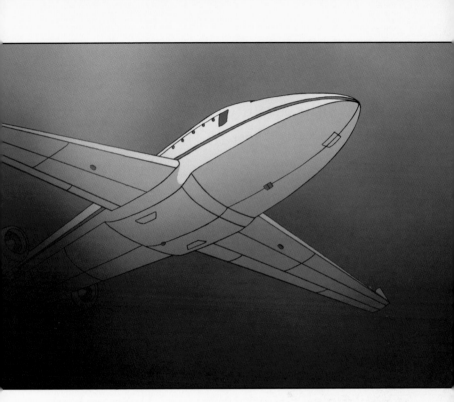

"Landing?" Mary-Kate asked. "Where?"

"Down there!" Ashley pointed to a thin airstrip in a beautiful green field.

"Fasten your seat belts, everyone!" Mary-Kate said. "I'm taking her down."

Ashley nodded. "Then it's off to Hedgemoor to stop Clive's evil plan!"

• • •

Moments later, Mary-Kate, Ashley, Rod, and Quincy were driving in the English countryside. Ashley carried a backpack.

"So, once we get to Hedgemoor, how are we going to get in without Clive seeing us?" Ashley asked.

"Don't worry. I have a plan," Mary-Kate said.

"It had better be good," Ashley warned. "This is serious business, Mary-Kate."

"I am serious!" Mary-Kate replied. "And we're supposed to use our code names when we're on assignment. Remember, Special Agent Amber?"

"Right," Ashley said. "Sorry, Special Agent Misty."

Rod turned off the main road and onto a long winding driveway. The car drove past a garden filled with tall plants and a maze made out of shrubbery.

Soon a huge stone mansion came into

view. It was so big, it looked like a castle!

"Here we are," Rod said. "Hedgemoor Manor. The house is on the northernmost point of the property. All the grounds are to the south."

"Thanks for the info, Rod," Mary-Kate said. She hopped out of the car.

"Wait!" Ashley called. "What's the plan?"

Mary-Kate smiled. "Just follow me."

# CHAPTER FOUR
## Mind Your Manor

Mary-Kate, Ashley, and Quincy climbed the large stone steps to the front door of Hedgemoor Manor.

"Digital diary: Four P.M. We are at the home of Clive Hedgemorton-Smythe," Mary-Kate whispered into her special-agent bracelet.

"Will you stop that?" Ashley asked. "You could blow our cover!" She scooped up Quincy and placed him in her backpack so he couldn't be seen.

"Quincy, you are not allowed to speak until we leave the mansion," Ashley said. "We don't want to look suspicious in any way."

"Got it," Quincy replied. He scrunched down in the backpack.

"Okay, here's the plan," Mary-Kate said. "When the butler comes to the door, we'll make up a reason he has to go get Clive. While he's away, we'll sneak in and look around."

"By the time he comes back, we'll be gone," Ashley added. "Excellent!"

Mary-Kate reached up and pressed the doorbell.

A short, round man answered. He was wearing a suit and a bow tie. "Good day,

my name is Simon. May I help you?" the
man asked. His mustache twitched as he
spoke.

Mary-Kate smiled. "Yes," she replied.
"Ummm, we're here for . . . the tour."

Simon frowned. "I'm sorry, there must
be some mistake," he said. "We do not
give tours. Good day." He began to close
the door.

Ashley quickly stuck her foot in the doorway. "Hold on," she said. "We saw an ad for this place on the Internet. We came really far to see it. We're not leaving until we get our tour!"

Simon stared down at Ashley's foot. "Very well." He sighed. "Please wait in the front hall while I check with Master Smythe."

Simon led Mary-Kate and Ashley into a large hallway with doors lining both sides. Then he hurried off.

"All right, Special Agent Amber, this is our chance," Mary-Kate said. "Let's search all these rooms for anything. And hurry— before Clive figures out that we're here!"

Ashley opened a door and peeked into a small room. All she saw was a couple of plants, a sofa, and a large painting in the corner. "Nothing weird in here," she called. "Did you find anything?"

Across the hall, Mary-Kate peered into a different room. "Just lots of hats and pictures of pale-faced ancestors. Clive is definitely not a man who likes to be in the sun."

"That doesn't explain why he'd want to ruin it for the rest of us," Ashley said.

Mary-Kate nodded. "We must be missing something."

Ashley paused. She heard footsteps down the hall. "Mary-Kate, do you hear that?"

"Someone's coming! Hide!" Mary-Kate whispered. She leaped into the room on her side of the hall and closed the door.

Ashley did the same on the other side of the hall.

The footsteps grew louder and louder.

Ashley's heart thumped in her chest. She could tell from all the footsteps that more than one person was walking by. Then the footsteps faded away.

*They must be gone*, Ashley thought. She opened the door. Mary-Kate was in the hall, waiting for her.

"That was close," Mary-Kate said. "Come on, let's keep searching."

Ashley glanced around. At the end of the hall, she spotted a set of heavy wooden doors. "That's the only room on this floor

we haven't searched," she said. "Let's go for it."

Ashley and Mary-Kate walked down the hall and pulled the doors open.

Mary-Kate stared into the room. "Hey! Look at all those books!"

"This must be the library," Ashley said. She walked over to a desk covered with papers and looked at the top one. "What do you think 'Password: Red Hot' means?" she asked, reading from one of the papers.

"That would be none of your business," a voice snapped.

Ashley spun around. Clive Hedgemorton-Smythe stood in the doorway. Simon stood beside him.

Ashley grabbed Mary-Kate's hand. They were caught!

# CHAPTER FIVE
## An A"maze"ing Mess

"What do we do?" Ashley whispered to Mary-Kate.

"Run!" Mary-Kate cried.

"Not so fast," Clive said. He blocked the doorway.

Ashley gulped. They were in trouble now.

Clive smiled, showing his cheese-covered teeth. "Once Simon described the American teenage girls who wanted a tour of my house, I knew it was the two of you!"

Clive waved the girls over. "Follow me," he said. "I'll give you a tour of this house that you'll never forget."

Ashley looked at Mary-Kate. Mary-Kate shrugged. "I don't think we have a choice," she said.

Clive picked up a plate of cheese from his desk. "Stilton?" he offered.

"Yuck! I mean, uh, none for me," Mary-Kate said.

"No, thanks." Ashley wrinkled her nose.

Clive grabbed a hunk of stinky cheese from the plate. He shoved it in his mouth. "All right, then, let's go." Clive marched out of the library, carrying the plate with him.

Ashley wanted to run the other way. But Simon was keeping a close eye on her and Mary-Kate.

Ashley sighed and followed Clive. Something caught her eye on her way out the door. One of the books on the bookshelf was crooked. All the others were perfectly straight.

Ashley reached out to straighten the book. But Simon stepped forward, blocking her.

"I'll see to that, miss," Simon said.

Ashley shrugged. Then she hurried to catch up with Clive.

"Where do you think he's taking us?" Mary-Kate whispered.

"I don't know," Ashley said. "But we'd better be careful."

• • •

"Where are we?" Ashley asked a few minutes later. Clive had led them outside and into the garden. They were surrounded by bushes that were at least ten feet high.

"This is my maze," Clive explained. He stuffed piece after piece of stinky cheese into his mouth as they walked.

When they had walked into the middle of the maze, Simon covered his nose and mouth with his hand. "I think it's time, sir," he said.

"Time for what?" Ashley asked.

Clive stepped closer and leaned toward Mary-Kate and Ashley. "For this!" he said. He breathed right in Mary-Kate's and Ashley's faces.

Ashley's stomach turned. Clive's breath was so horrible, she could barely breathe.

"What's happening?" Ashley asked weakly. The world swam before her eyes.

Then everything went dark.

# CHAPTER SIX
# Wish Upon a Star

Ashley felt something wet and cold on her face. She opened her eyes. It was Quincy! He was licking her cheek with his tongue.

"All right!" Quincy said. "I've been trying to wake you up forever. Good thing I was able to get out of your backpack!"

Ashley sat up. Quincy began licking Mary-Kate's face.

"Wh-where are we?" Mary-Kate asked as she opened her eyes.

"Still in Clive's maze," Quincy said.

Ashley stared at the sky. It was nighttime now. Above her, millions of stars twinkled. "Wow!" she said. "Clive's breath was so bad, it knocked us out for hours!"

"We have to find our way out of here and stop Clive before it's too late," Mary-Kate said.

"Quincy's computer should be able to tell us which way to go," Mary-Kate added. She pushed a button on Quincy's collar.

Quincy was quiet for a moment. "Hmmm. I'm not getting a signal," he said.

"We can use our bracelets instead," Ashley suggested.

Mary-Kate pressed a button on her special-agent bracelet. "The screen is all fuzzy," she said. "I can't see what it says."

Ashley switched on her own bracelet. Static filled its tiny screen. "Something must be blocking the signal."

"We're completely gadgetless!" Mary-Kate cried. "What do we do now?"

"Wait a minute!" Ashley said. "I know how to get us out of here."

"You do?" Mary-Kate asked.

Ashley nodded. "The answer was in our astronomy homework. Remember how Rod said the house was on the northernmost point of the estate?"

"Yeah, so?" Mary-Kate said.

"So all we have to do is keep our eye on the North Star and it will lead us back to the house!"

"And we know the North Star is the biggest, brightest star in the sky," Mary-Kate added.

"There it is." Ashley pointed to a bright twinkle of light. "Follow me!"

• • •

A few minutes later, Ashley sneaked into Clive's mansion. Mary-Kate and Quincy followed close behind. The house was dark and quiet.

"Where are Clive and Simon?" Mary-Kate whispered.

"I'm not sure," Ashley answered. "But I think we should take another look at those papers in the library."

They tiptoed down the hall and into Clive's library. Ashley walked straight to the desk at the far end of the room. She picked up one of the papers.

"What do you think this is?" Mary-Kate asked, staring at the drawing on the page.

Ashley pointed to two round objects. "Well, this is Earth. And this looks like the sun. This thing in the middle could be—"

"A satellite!" Mary-Kate finished. "And look, it's sending out a force field to block the sun's rays."

Mary-Kate flipped to the next page. "Hey, check this out!"

Ashley stared at the drawing and gasped. "Cheesebreath built a rocket ship! And it looks like he could live on it! Is he planning to leave the earth?"

"That would make sense," Mary-Kate

pointed out. "Once the sun is blocked out, we will all freeze. Clive has to leave, or he will freeze, too."

"Then, if we keep him from escaping, he won't block out the sun!" Ashley said.

"Right," Mary-Kate agreed. "But where would Clive keep a rocket ship around here?"

Ashley's eyes fell on the crooked book on the shelf. "Maybe he keeps it in a secret passageway," she said. "And I bet I know how to find it!"

Ashley ran over to the book and straightened it.

"What's the password?" a mechanical voice asked.

Ashley looked at Mary-Kate.

Mary-Kate shrugged. "I don't know what it is," she said.

"Well, *I* do!" Ashley replied. "It's written right on the papers!"

Mary-Kate shook her head. "No way. Not even Clive is that dumb!"

"What's the password?" the voice asked again.

"Ummm, red hot?" Ashley guessed.

*Whooosh!* The bookcase slid away to reveal a staircase. Mary-Kate and Ashley smiled at each other.

"Wow, he actually *is* that dumb!" Mary-Kate joked.

"Come on, girls," Quincy said. "Let's go!"

# CHAPTER SEVEN
## Countdown to Disaster

Ashley raced down the stairs. When she reached the bottom, she was standing in front of a huge rocket ship!

"Whoa! Now this is getting interesting," Mary-Kate said.

Ashley pulled IQ's lipstick and earring walkie-talkies from her backpack. "We can't sneak into the rocket ship. Clive and Simon will see us."

"But maybe they won't notice Quincy," Mary-Kate said.

Ashley twisted the base of the lipstick to the on position, then tossed the lipstick to Quincy. "If Quincy sneaks in with the lipstick, we'll be able to hear Clive through these earrings!"

Quincy nodded. He caught the lipstick and ran into the rocket.

Ashley handed Mary-Kate one of the earrings. Soon they heard Clive's voice through the earrings' speakers.

"Well, it looks like all systems are ready," he said.

"Yes, sir," Simon answered. "I've stocked the ship with plenty of cheese. We had so much in the house, I had to leave some behind."

"Very good," Clive said. "Did you pack sunscreen just in case we ever have to leave the rocket ship?"

"Of course," Simon said. "Super-strength."

"You can't be too careful when you have fair skin like mine, Simon," Clive said. "Sunbathers don't understand that. They always make fun of me with my gallons of sunscreen."

"Yes, sir," Simon agreed.

"I hate that," Clive said. "'Pasty Clive, barely alive, needs a sun hat to survive.'

Well, we'll see who is more pasty after I block out the sun!"

Ashley turned to Mary-Kate. "Gee, I feel kind of bad that Clive gets teased so much."

"Yeah." Mary-Kate shrugged. "But it's no excuse to destroy the earth!"

Quincy ran out of the rocket. "Better hurry, girls!" he said. "Clive is beginning his final countdown!"

A rumbling sound filled the air. Ashley saw a huge door in the ceiling begin to open.

"What are we going to do?" Mary-Kate asked.

Ashley looked around. A few feet away, dozens of cheese wheels were stacked on top of one another.

"That's it!" Ashley exclaimed. "We'll stuff the cheese in the rocket's engine. Then it won't be able to take off!"

"T minus ten seconds to liftoff," a computerized voice announced.

Mary-Kate and Ashley moved quickly, stuffing the giant wheels of cheese into the rocket ship's engine. The voice continued the countdown. "T minus four, three, two . . ."

*Rooooar!* The ship began to take off.

"Hide!" Ashley shouted. The girls and Quincy dove behind a stack of big wooden crates.

*KA-BOOM!* The rocket ship exploded, splashing gooey melted cheese everywhere.

Clive and Simon stumbled out of the rocket. They fell in a heap at Mary-Kate's and Ashley's feet.

"You ruined my plan!" Clive cried.

"News flash," Mary-Kate replied. "If you thought you were too pale, you didn't have to destroy the world. All you had to do was use some self-tanner!"

"It colors your skin like a real tan, and you don't have to go in the sun," Ashley added.

Clive blinked. "Simon!" he yelled. "How come you never told me about self-tanner?"

"Don't worry, Clive," Mary-Kate said. "We'll send you some while you're in the slammer!"

She flipped open her special-agent bracelet. "Headquarters," she announced, "our mission is over. Agents Misty and Amber have saved the world."

Ashley giggled. "Again!"

FROM: Special Agents Misty and Amber
TO: All Mary-Kate and Ashley Fans
LOCATION: Around the World
YOUR MISSION: Collect all the books in the
series and join us as we save the world from
super-villains who are out to cause trouble!

## LET'S GO SAVE THE WORLD... AGAIN!

Find out what is causing the
fashion model meltdown!

Are the Hipslovian gymnasts
a perfect ten—or just
perfect cheaters?

Go undercover to solve
a sticky mess!

Stop the world from
turning into a desert!

Sniff out what's going on
at the Bot Puppy factory!

How will Misty and Amber
stop Capital D from taking
over the airwaves?

# mary-kateandashley

## Hang out with Mary-Kate and Ashley in these cool books and find out...

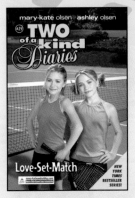

...if co-ed sleepaway camp will be a bust—or a blast?

...how Mary-Kate and Ashley juggle all their activities and still find time for each other!

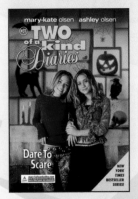

...what happens when Mary-Kate and Ashley help out with the Haunted House this Halloween!

## BASED ON THE HIT TELEVISION SERIES!

It's
What
YOU
Read.

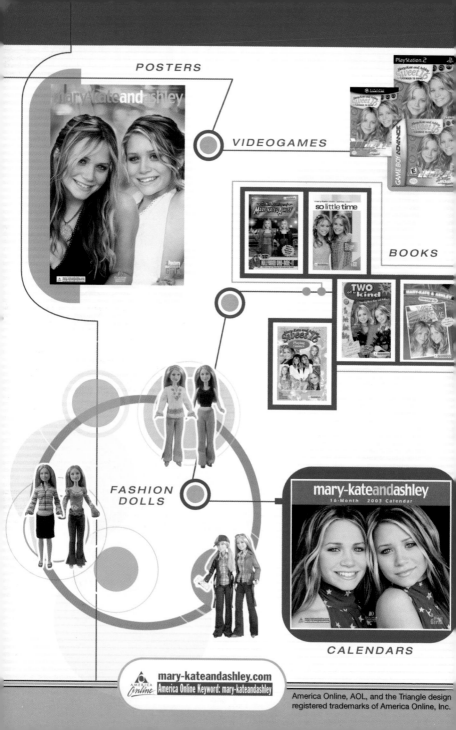

POSTERS

VIDEOGAMES

BOOKS

FASHION DOLLS

CALENDARS

mary-kateandashley
16-Month 2003 Calendar